HALF PENNY'S REVENGE

By

Lennon Joseph

This novel is entirely a work of fiction. The names, characters and incidents portrayed in it are the work of the author's imagination. Any resemblance to actual persons, living or dead, events or localities is entirely coincidental. Lennon Joseph asserts the moral right to be identified as the author of this work.

Lennon Joseph has no responsibility for the persistence or accuracy of URLs for external or third-party Internet Websites referred to in this publication and does not guarantee that any content on such Websites is, or will remain, correct or appropriate.

If you enjoyed Half Penny's Revenge or any other books in the series, please leave a review so others can hear what you thought. Perhaps more importantly, I would love to hear if you liked the book, and what you liked? Thank you.

Contents

Chapter 1

AN URGENT MEETING

I t was a rainy and cloudy night over Dark Woods. Jacob was in his house in the woods of Dark Woods, sitting by the fireplace and trying to stay warm, because it seemed even his warm clothes were not keeping him warm tonight. He held a photo he had taken out of a little box in his hands, the same box where he stored his books and diaries. His seated figure threw a sinister dancing shadow against the background of the living room because he had switched off the lights except the firelight and the LSD lamp that stood near the fireplace. He was staring sadly at the photo of him and the girl, which he had found earlier.

This evening, he had been doing some research as he tried to get more information about its magic and more about Halloween night, and how all these things tied in with the monsters that were contained in his books - some of which had been released and caused so much harm to Dark Woods and to him and his friends. How, he wondered, did it allow Half Penny and every monster to escape at once even though the books didn't work like that? The thunder and lightning began to unleash their fury with booming sounds and such bright flashes that for half a second it seemed brighter than midday. Sometimes the wind would blow so hard the windows shook and it seemed as if the roof would be lifted off the house. An ordinary boy

1

would have been scared to be alone in the house in the woods on a stormy night, but Jacob was no ordinary boy.

As Jacob was studying his blood and about dark magic powers, something he heard on the TV made him turn around. He had not been paying much attention to the TV until now.

"We would like to warn our viewers that the next bit of news may sound bizarre and disturbing. A man died this evening under very mysterious circumstances. The eye witness has been interviewed by the police. He was the last person to see the dead man alive. According to this eye witness, the man collapsed right in front of him and his face and chest were full of blood, and yet his attacker or the cause of the attack was not visible to the bystander. The witness says that the deceased's last words were: 'Help; I saw a puppet with this pale creepy face, and he appeared from a book - first as a picture and then as a real-life creature. He clawed my face and chest...I'm dying.' The shock of this incident, especially as the witness saw this man collapse in a pool of blood but could not see the attacker, has had a serious Impact on the mental state of the witness, who has been sent to the Raven Sparrows Mental Hospital for protection from the world. The police insist that the so-called witness is actually the murderer and must have murdered the deceased. His story and his behaviour led to the conclusion that the witness has acute mental issues and could pose a serious danger to the society, something the witness' family vehemently denies. The picture book the dead man mentioned was not found anywhere."

Jacob froze. He was terrified that this time they were all in absolute danger; not just Jacob and his friends but other residents of the town of Dark Woods. If the dead man had described the assailant as a puppet, it could only mean one thing: Half Penny! No one would believe the witness except Jacob and his friends, who had encountered Half Penny before. Their sadistic, deadly nemesis was back. What would he do this time around? He had warned Jacob and his friends earlier that he would not only destroy them but that he had wicked plans for the entire town of Dark Woods.

Jacob decided to call Amelia, the little girl who had now become a part of Jack's family and who had been found in the woods around that Halloween time (see Book 1). Jacob did not need to go to the phone and ring her up and go through the Inconvenience of waking everybody up. His eyes and hands began to glow in purple and black flames, and he telepathically called in his mental projection. Meanwhile in Amelia's bedroom all was quiet except for the storm raging outside. She was asleep and then she realized that Jacob was in her dream. He appeared to be sitting near the curtain in her bedroom, but she could tell he was back inside his house in the woods.

"Jacob. What are you doing? What do you want?" she asked.

He replied, "Amelia I need to talk to you."

"Okay, what is it?" Amelia asked.

"Meet me in the treehouse tomorrow and tell Jack to come with you, okay?"

Amelia agreed to it. "Is that all? Can I go to sleep now?"

"Yes." And Jacob seemed to vanish.

In the morning Jacob woke up and got dressed. As he was eating breakfast, he watched his memories with his mind holographs and was upset over something. He was ready to go meet up with the others. He stepped outside the house and then turned and stared at it, and then used his magic and turned it invisible and moved the house somewhere else in the woods. Now it seemed as if he was standing all alone in the woods. In fact, a man and a woman walking around the woods stopped and stared at him, wondering what he was doing all alone in the woods.

"Are you alright Son? Are you alone?" the man asked.

"Are you lost?" asked the woman. Jacob turned and locked eyes with them, and the paused, shocked by the intense look in his eyes. Just then he used his secret powers and teleported them to the outskirts of Dark Woods and wiped away their memories of seeing him in the woods. They would wake up and wonder why they had slept out there.

Jacob was soon walking through the woods on his way to the treehouse to talk to everyone about what has happened recently in Dark Woods.

Meanwhile back in the Tickers' house Tom, Eliot, Jack, Amelia and Luna were playing a video game. Luna was the girl they had met when they were trying to solve the mystery of the deadly scarecrows that Half Penny had used to wreak havoc on Dark Woods (see Book 2). As Jacob teleported close to the neighbourhood, he turned invisible to keep away prying eyes. One rider who had been riding behind Jacob nearly fell off his bike when he noticed that the boy who had been only ten metres ahead had suddenly vanished, and he had no idea where he had gone and there was a wall on both sides. Jacob walked to the Tickers' house and knocked on the door and said hello to Tom and Eliot's mom.

Mrs Ticker smiled. "Oh, hello Jacob; how are you?" Jacob smiled. "Hello Mrs Ticker, I'm okay. Um, are Eliot and Tom here? I need to see them."

4

Mr Ticker nodded. "They are in the treehouse you kids go to sometimes. Or perhaps they are planning to go there." She chuckled. "Nice to see you by the way."

Jacob snickered. "Pleased to see you today too, Mrs Ticker."

As he walked slowly upstairs and entered the room and said hello to his friends, they were all very happy to see him that day, but they noticed that something seemed to be troubling him. His smile appeared a little forced and he seemed to have a lot on his mind. There was no0ne of that mischievous twinkle in his eyes.

"Guys, can we have a meeting in the treehouse? This is important."

Tom asked: "Okay, Jacob; should we go get Lucy?"

Jacob said, "Yeah, just hurry and get her."

Tom rushed into Lucy's room and asked her to come to the treehouse, but she had her eyes glued to a book. She sighed and replied "Leave me alone," and she almost shut the door on him. Then he said to her, "Half Penny is out of his book!!!" Now he had caught her attention and she looked scared. But she said she couldn't because she had to go to the Dark Woods city hall to make sure there weren't any more books there and Tom agreed, and he would call her if they found anything too.

Tom and Eliot had made a proper little house up in the huge tree and even nailed a bench where they could sit and even fitted two wooden chairs up in the tree. Tom had tied a large tarpaulin paper above to keep away the rain if it ever rained while they were up in the treehouse.

As soon as Luna and Amelia arrived, the boys and the girls headed for the treehouse. In the meeting in the treehouse Jacob explained that

Half Penny had been released from his book and killed someone and it had been on the news.

"We have to find that monster and trap it at all costs before more people die!" he finished. Then he turned to Luna and asked: "Luna, have you got your powers under control?" and she enviously replied "Well, not really, not like you do. I don't know how to use it at all and when I try to teleport, I just end up burning down a tree."

Jacob replied, "Well, both Amelia and I have powers - maybe we could go to the forest and give you lessons on how to control your powers by choice; will that help?" Jack asked, "Why do we have to?" He was thinking of all the terrible things that had happened to them before out there in the forest.

Jacob explained: "Well, we do need all the help we can get and if three of us can use our powers properly that will be better than just two of us."

Chapter 2

A NEW ENEMY

They all agreed to the plan. Before they left, they told Mrs Ticker that they were just going to the forest to play, and they would be back by night time. As they were cycling to the forest, they found themselves near House No 1231 on Black Hill where Tom and Eliot had found the "Horror Halloween" book last year.

Jacob seemed very quiet and very thoughtful about being back there. They saw a police car and three police officers in the front yard when they stopped at the gate. The police seemed to be searching for something, perhaps clues, but the friends were not sure what exactly they were looking for.

"Hey, kids, what are you doing there?" one burly officer yelled at them. "This place is out of bounds!"

"What is going on?" Jacob asked. "Why are you searching the house?"

The police officer replied: "Well, kids; we think that this place should be renovated, and we have a suspicion that this place could be somehow connected to the Halloween attack last year and you kids should get going because everyone in Dark Woods thinks this place is haunted."

Tom yelled: "Yes, but not us," as they all cycled away deep into the forest. When they stopped inside what seemed like a small clearing surrounded by thick trees, Eliot asked "Um, Jacob, how are we going to stop people from seeing Luna's powers?" The others agreed that this was a good question.

Jacob channelled his powers, and his pale hands and black eyes emitted purple and black flames and he put a force field around the area where they were standing, and he explained that if people showed up, they couldn't see or hear them, and they couldn't even feel them.

Jacob then turned to Luna. "Okay, Luna; can tell me what you can do using your powers?"

Luna frowned. "Well, I can set stuff on fire, I can teleport, turn invisible, I can even move stuff with my mind, and I can control people."

Amelia gaped. "Wow, and do you have control over when to do these things or does it happen on its own?"

Luna said, "Well, usually when I want to do something they happen there on, and it's very, very frustrating."

Jacob nodded in agreement. "Yeah, when I first got my powers, I was eight years old, and it was very frustrating. One time I almost blew my house to ash when I got mad. So maybe we should see you in action."

The group looked at each other in shock on hearing that Jacob got his powers when he was only eight years old. Luna replied: "Uh, okay." As Jacob and Luna began shooting powers at each other and dodging, he even showed her that her powers were based on her emotions, and some were mental. As he shot her with his powers, she was able to dodge but couldn't avoid his blast of magic waves.

Jacob said, "Pyrokinesis, telekinesis, teleportation, electrogenesis and super speed are very hard powers to use. Don't let your desires and

8

emotions get in the way of your concentration, okay?" He grabbed her hand and lifted her from the ground and asked her if she had pain absorbing powers and she said she was not sure. Jacob said that if she had that she could be immune to pain and could protect herself against anything.

Luna was getting angry because she hated being hurt. Jacob shot a fireball at her, and she was severely injured. She and the group were furious at him and blamed him for hurting her, but before he could apologize, he was cornered at the tree and Amelia and everyone else began hurting him saying horribly cruel things to him at the same time. When he growled and became really enraged, he became increasingly overwhelmed. His whole body and eyes began to spark, buzz and then emit purple and black flames and he screamed and yelled "stop it!!!!" A huge energy burst emitted from him and threw everyone into the air to the trees. Tom felt as if an invisible hand had grabbed him and thrown him back into the branches of a tree. Amelia was being thrown towards the trunk of a tree at a terrific force, but she was able to counter this force and fell only a few feet away. Eliot and Luna lay on the grass near the trees.

Everyone was groaning as they felt as if an invisible wall was pushing against their chests and as nursed bruises. Jacob was panting.

Amelia shouted: "Why did you do that? Jerk."

Jacob snapped: "Don't you ever speak to me like that, okay?!!!"

Luna was furious. "That's it!"

At that very moment Luna, Amelia and Jacob began to brutally attack each other with each of their powers, but they were all an equal match and almost killed each other at the same time. Jacob and the others were however shocked that Amelia and Luna had just about as much power as Jacob, even though they rarely used these powers. As Jacob had a psychotic breakdown, he threatened to send them all to the Mirror Dimension, but after that he realized that he had almost done a terrible thing with his magic and regretted this. Luna and Amelia, both blasted him with their powers and Jacob released a huge energy ring that made a huge wind blow to the trees, and he yelled at them: "Enough! Listen, don't bother trying to stop the darkness from coming, because I'll do this on my own so don't look for me!" and Jacob teleported away to unknown parts. The group were angry and sad and upset at him, and they all walked back to the Tickers' house. Their sombre moods and silence made Mr and Mrs Ticker ask their two sons and their friends what was wrong, but they only replied: "Let's just say that Jacob is no longer our friend, and we just want to be alone, okay?"

Mrd Ticker seemed concerned, but she shrugged. "Okay, but we can tell something is troubling you all." Eliot said: "Okay, Mom, Jacob just got mad, and he hurt us and we're not friends anymore, okay? So we just want to be alone."

Luna sat angrily in the corner. A resentment for Jacob was growing inside her. Amelia was equally angry, but she was a person who always tried to make peace, therefore she was trying to figure out what possible reason Jacob could have had for doing what he had done and she was wondering: had they misunderstood him? Amelia was a peaceful person; she never let anger get the best of her and most importantly, she never got violent. Not once in a million years had she ever thought she would try to use her powers against any of her friends. As someone who always kept her frustration in check, Amelia

10

was disappointed in herself for the part she had played in the fight. She thought of all the things she could have done differently to calm the situation, and a fresh swell of rage rose within her.

Why had she not taken the high road and tried to calm things down, she thought angrily to herself. Throughout their history of friendship, this was the biggest fight the kids had ever had amongst themselves, and this one was the most dangerous because they had been using powers beyond their natural human powers and could have hurt each other badly, or even hurt Tom or Eliot. Amelia decided to go grab a cup of water just to try and calm down.

Luna sat by the kitchen counter with her hands dipped in a bowl of ice. Her hands were slightly swollen from the fight that had ensued earlier with Jacob.

"I have a terrible migraine, I feel like my head is about to explode or something," Amelia moaned.

"Personally it is my eyes, I am still trying to adjust my focus. Jacob did a number on me with that intense surge of light," Luna complained.

"Gosh, me too! He did not play fair with that light spell. It blinded me for a second back there," Amelia added.

"But I am glad we ended it before someone got seriously hurt. Though I must say I am still so enraged with Jacob. I can't even stand to see him right now," Luna exclaimed.

The two girls fell into mutual ominous silence. They were each lost in their thoughts and wondering what that fight would mean for their friendship. Tom and Eliot followed the girls into the kitchen.

"A penny for your thoughts," Eliot said to Luna and startled her in the process.

11

"Absolutely not, I'll save them for a dollar," Luna replied cheekily.

"You guys looked like you are brooding over something in this kitchen," Tom observed when he saw their sullen faces.

"The death of our friendship with Jacob, maybe," Luna replied. "Or realizing that we can hurt each other badly if we chose to."

"Guys, let us not be rushed in passing judgements. It is never a good idea to make decisions when emotional. What happened earlier was an unfortunate incident, but Jacob is still our good friend," Amelia explained.

"You are right, let us all take some time to cool down and then we can decide what to do," Tom said.

"I know just the thing to cheer us up. Let's go upstairs and play board games!" Eliot suggested excitedly.

It sounded like a swell idea, so they all walked upstairs to play the game. They settled on playing chess, which happened to be Eliot's favourite. Eliot set up the game and the pawn exchange began. In the first round, he played against Luna, who was quite poor in the game. Two minutes in, she sacrificed her black night for position which opened her up for an attack. Eliot was more than ready to take advantage of the opening and it didn't take long before he had won the game. It was not until the two chess pros faced off in an intense round that the game got a little interesting. Amelia was also a chess queen in her own right. She liked to carefully calculate her moves. She started with her favourite, the queen's gambit. Soon after she took control of the centre board and was running the show. Eliot put on a good fight; he refused to take the bait that Amelia kept placing for him. His defence was pretty strong; this was going to be a long game.

Tom decided to go make himself a snack because the way things were going, they were going to be a long time there.

Chapter 3

AN OLD FRIEND

Meanwhile, a large dark cloud was beginning to engulf the dead desolate forest of Dark Woods. The now-dead plants and vines danced and swayed from side to side in the gentle breeze. A shadowy, human-shaped figure emerged from the blanket of the trees. It was Jacob. His hair was wet from running across the forest and brushing past the dew in the branches. He had a forbidding look on his face and looked pretty glum. He was heaving loudly from the run. He sat by one of the branches of the tree and took a long deep breath. He felt tired, exhausted, frustrated and angry. He had never meant for things to take a turn for the worst. He had reflected on his actions, and he felt terrible for letting his anger get the best of him. But worse than that, he felt deeply betrayed by his friends. They all ganged up against him; not even one person took his side or tried to reason things out with him. He started mumbling and grumbling about Luna, Amelia, Tom, and Eliot and how horrible they were being to him.

"You know what, I don't even need them. I will stop Half Penny on my own. Who needs a bunch of immature whiny kids," he scoffed. "They do not even realize what is at stake here; the fate of Dark Woods is in our hands, and they are still picking fights!"

The more he thought about it the angrier he got. At this point, he could not even recognize the part he had played in antagonizing his friends. He thought back to the days when everyone got along and always solved their problems together. He remembered how they used to cover for each other to their parents when one was in trouble. They would often sneak off to play and hold tea parties in Tom's yard. His mom made the best homemade cookies, so it was always fun to play at their home. Sometimes the kids would stay longer than their parents allowed but as long as they were at each other's homes their parents understood.

Jacob thought about this bond they shared and thought it was sad that now they may never be friends anymore. Ever since Halloween, tension had mounted amongst the kids. They had been forced to grow up faster than they should. Another thing that brought undue tension amongst them was the power play. Jacob got his powers first and it was kind of fun being the one the kids looked up to. Then they met Amelia and with time her powers were revealed more and more, and now Luna had them too. At first, it did not bother Jacob that the others had powers too, but now there seemed to be a power struggle on who can do what and whose powers were stronger than the other. Jacob still wanted to maintain his hold as the leader of the group but now he was facing opposition from Luna and Amelia, or that is what he perceived to be the case. Little did he know that Luna and Amelia had no intention of being leaders in the group; the girls only wanted to use their powers for good and to stop Half Penny. But Jacob was too self-absorbed to realize that.

Thinking back to the good old days made him remember an old friend he had not heard from in two years. Her name was Cloe Samson; her mother and his mother had been best friends when he was born. Cloe was only a few months older than him, but they both

15

grew to form a very tight bond. Their mothers often organized joint playdates for the kids to enjoy. Cloe and Jacob got along pretty well from the start, and most people who did not know them well assumed they were siblings because they were always together. However, when he was three years old, Jacob's father got a job in Dark Woods and the family had to relocate. The relocation was much harder on Jacob because he was leaving his closest and most personal friend Cloe. Their parents tried to help them keep in touch by visiting each other and sending birthday and Christmas cards and gifts. As they got older, they would also make phone calls to each other and always knew what was going on in each other's life.

However, for two years now these two bosom friends had neither spoken nor seen each other. The cards stopped coming in or going out and the phone stopped ringing. Jacob filled the void with his newfound friends in Dark Woods and with time the memories of Cloe vanished. Well, that was until now. His fight with his friends had reminded her of the only other friend he had and could count on. Besides, Cloe had shared with him that she also had received powers that she was trying to navigate how to use them. This made Cloe perfect to help out with the mission to find Half Penny and get rid of him – hopefully for good this time. Since Jacob wasn't sure if they still lived at the same address or if they had relocated, he decided to go home and ask his friend Jim's mother. Jim and his mom had been neighbours when Jacob and his parents moved to Dark Woods. But Jim wasn't home – only his mother was.

He found Jim's mother in the kitchen preparing dinner. The aroma of fried chicken wafted in the air. Jacob's stomach growled. He had been so preoccupied with the fight that he had forgotten to take lunch. Now he felt the pangs of hunger gnawing him.

"Hello, Cloe's Mom, this smells amazing," Jacob said.

"Sit down, I'll fix you a plate," Cloe's mom offered. "We rarely see you anymore, Jacob. Jim is at his uncle's in Manchester and won't be back for days. It's late; you can stay the night. How are your parents doing? Didn't they leave Dark Woods?"

"Yes, they did," Jacob said, but said no more about that.

"Are you staying at Jack's or Tom and Eliot's place?"

"I stay with Tom and Eliot mostly," he said, but did not say that he never spent the night there.

As Cloe's mom went about fixing him a plate, she started making small talk with him.

"So what have you been up to today?"

"Nothing much; just hanging out with my friends," Jacob replied.

"So nothing happened that you want to talk about?" his mother prodded.

"Nope, nothing," Jacob replied as he started eating his fried chicken.

"Well, I received a call from Mrs Ticker earlier. She told me you and the kids were involved in a fight. Can you explain to me what happened?" she asked.

"Eliot!" Jacob muttered under his teeth. He knew Eliot was the tell-tale.

"What did you say?" she asked.

"I said I am sorry. It was just a stupid fight that blew out of proportion…more than it should have. But I will fix things later," Jacob explained quickly to get her off his case.

"You'd better," she replied.

Jacob enjoyed the scrumptious meal. He cleared the table once he was done and even placed the dirty utensils in the dishwasher. Jim's mother even let him speak to Jim at his uncle's place.

Now was the perfect opportunity to ask where Cloe lived.

"Does Cloe and her parents still live down at 2904 Black Hill?" Jacob asked.

"Yes, they sure do; wow, you haven't asked me about Cloey in such a long time.

"Well, I haven't talked to her in a long time, but I want to change that. I'll go see her early tomorrow morning," Jacob replied.

That night Jacob lay awake in bed for quite a long time. He could not stop thinking about how Cloey would receive him. It had been his fault because they had lost touch with each other, and he felt like she would be angry at him.

The next morning Jacob was woken up by the glistening rays of the sun beaming through his blinds. He sat up quickly thinking he had slept through his alarm but upon checking he realized he was five minutes early. The smell of fried bacon wafted in the air and Jacob instantly remembered he had spent the night at Jim's place. You could hear the sizzling of the bacon and the familiar scent of maple syrup. Despite the enticing smell, Jacob felt he needed to get to Cloe's house without wasting any time. He said goodbye to Jim's mom and thanked her and promised he would eat later.

He cycled down the road but as soon as he was out of sight, he used his powers to send the bike to his house in the woods, and then he teleported to the once familiar place: 2904 Black Hill. The area made him feel deeply nostalgic for all the times we spent playing on the pavements will Cloey and other friends. He regretted that it had taken him this long to come down this path but never better late than never, right?

Jacob arrived at the house. The gate was open - as if someone had just left the compound. He went up to the front door. He pressed the doorbell and three minutes later someone opened the door. The girl standing at the door had black and red eyes, a pale skin and short, black hair with one strip of purple on the left. It was Cloe Samson. She gaped at him, and her eyebrows went up in surprise before her face split into a wide smile. Jacob could not help but notice that she had grown taller in the two years since he last saw her.

"Well, well, well – look what the cat dragged in," Cloe said and laughed. Then she gave him a warm hug.

Cloe invited Jacob into the house; the two friends had a lot to catch up about. They talked endlessly and enjoyed great laughs in between. Jacob told Cloe about everything, including their fight against Half Penny. He told her all about the horrendous things that Half Penny had done to the people of Dark Woods and why he needed to be stopped.

"This is also part of the reason why I came to you today, I need your help in stopping Half Penny," Jacob said.

"You know I would love to help, but if you don't mind me asking, what happened to your friends back in Dark Woods? Aren't they the ones who always help you fight Half Penny?" Cloe asked out of curiosity.

"We had a fight; we are currently not on speaking terms," Jacob answered.

"I am sorry to hear that. I hope it was nothing serious," Cloe said, genuinely concerned.

"We will get past this, don't worry," Jacob reassured her. "Anyway, can we go somewhere a little more private? I need to discuss something a little more sensitive with you."

"Yeah, sure, let us go to the forest house," Cloe suggested.

Chapter 4

A DANGEROUS MISSION

Jacob and Cloe teleported away to Jacob's house in the forest. It was Cloe that teleported them away. Jacob was quite impressed by how much control she had over her powers. She used them with so much ease.

"Have you been practising and experimenting with your powers?" Jacob asked curiously.

"Yeah, one time I almost burnt down our house out of anger. That is when I realized my power can be destructive if I don't learn how to control them. Since that day when I am free, I come out here in the forest, create a force field then practise," Cloe replied proudly.

"Wow, I am so impressed. I had to learn how to control my powers the hard way – fighting Half Penny. Anyway, it is good that you took the initiative to learn how to control your powers yourself," Jacob said.

"So what did you want to talk to me about?" Cloe asked.

"I've got some bad news; I fear that Half penny is on the loose again. I saw on the news two days ago about how he killed a man in a valley and the other victims said the dead man said the monster appeared from a magic book. The reports say the man was so traumatized that he is now being held in a Dark Woods mental asylum," Jacob explained.

"Oh my goodness! That is so terrible. The things that man saw must have been so terrible. Poor thing!" Cloe said sympathetically.

21

"I know. When the police found him, he was so traumatized that he was mumbling words and looked to be so out of touch with reality. They are helping him at the mental institution, but the police also think he may have murdered the dead man because the story of a mysterious puppet-like creature is a story the police are not ready to believe. You see the problem? Nobody but my friends and I, including you, know that Half Penny really exists, and most people would never believe us."

"So what are we going to do about Half Penny?"

"I am still thinking about a plan, stopping Half Penny is not going to be easy," Jacob moaned.

"If we stopped him once, then we can stop him again," Cloe replied confidently.

"It's not that easy we had the book last time and who knows what happened to Half Penny's book when he was released," Jacob said sadly.

"We will figure out a way," Cloe reassured him.

Later that day, Jacob and Cloe went back to Cloe's house. They needed to come up with a plan on how to stop Half Penny. Cloe fixed them a snack as they sat on the porch. They started bouncing off ideas to see what would be the best way to handle and outwit Half Penny.

"Maybe we can use the same method we used to stop him the last time we tried," Cloe suggested.

"I don't think it works like that, Cloe; every journal comes with a different principle," Jacob explained.

"Okay, if that is the case then we need to look for the book that releases Half Penny. We need to go back to where this incident happened. If we do not find the book maybe we can find clues that will help us," Cloe said.

" That's actually a brilliant idea," Jacob said, impressed.

By this time, darkness had started creeping in on the land, suffocating everything it touched in the process. The birds were moving back to their nests and so were the many residents of Dark Woods. Traffic was already pretty heavy by this time.

"If there is one thing, I am grateful for it is that I do not have to deal with traffic anymore. I can just teleport to wherever I want to go," Cloe said cheerfully.

"You are right about that. Sometimes I ride on my bike just for the exercise, but teleporting is so much fun," Jacob agreed with her.

Jacob and Cloe teleported themselves to the wooded area where Half Penny was released. The place had been sealed by the police officers because it was considered an active crime scene and an open case that was still under investigation. If the police officers were there, they would not have been allowed to get past the barriers but at this hour the police had already left. However, they were utterly shocked to see that there were two seemingly dead bodies in an area that had already been sealed off by the police. Jacob was sure that whoever had dumped the bodies there had done so after the police had left. His fears were soon confirmed when they noticed that the two bodies were covered with a mask on their faces that read: "Happy reunion, Jacob and Cloe!"

Cloe was totally shaken by this. *How had Half Penny known that they were going to visit the crime scene? And most importantly, how had he known that she and Jacob had reunited after all these years? Was he stalking them? Had he been watching them this whole time?* Cloe's mind raced with thoughts. A tinge of fear gripped her and for the first time that day she felt really scared. Perhaps this was something even Jacob could not handle. As for her, despite having power, she had never had to go head-on with Half Penny, and she was not sure of what to expect.

"Hey, don't be scared Cloe," Jacob said to her when he noticed her hesitation; "These are just one of Half Penny's antics to scare us. He feeds off people's fear, so don't give him the satisfaction."

This made Cloe feel a little more confident. She stepped forward and pulled the bags off the men's bodies. What they saw made Cloe want to throw up, but she didn't. The men had been brutally murdered in the most gruesome way. Their eyes had been stabbed with pieces of broken light bulbs. They had several cuts on their faces running down to their neck. The murderer had cut the major artery on the neck and that was the cause of the pool of blood that was surrounding the bodies. Their legs had been broken and were facing a very unnatural and weird angel. It looked like a scene from a horror show, the one where nobody makes it out. Jacob knew Half Penny had intended for them to find the bodies like this to spook them. He had succeeded in his mission as Cloe and Jacob were starting to get spooked by the bloody and messy scene in front of them.

"Gosh, you have to be really sick to kill someone in this manner," Cloe said disgustedly.

"He is a monster," Jacob added.

Just as he finished making this statement, they heard the rustling of leaves behind them. They immediately knew they were not alone. Cloe felt a chilling fear take over her body. A human-shaped ghoul emerged from the thick blanket of trees and was making its way toward them. It had ruby red eyes that gleamed like the red dot from a sniper rifle. His eyes were like giant red exoplanets glowing in the galaxy. Jacob and Cloe did not wait to face this monster of a man, not today at least. They decided to use super speed to run away before whatever that was could kill them. They ran back to Jacobs's house in the forest.

"That was very horrifying. Even worse than the last time I saw something like this," Cloe said, panting.

"Not to me, I have seen enough horrifying creatures like this. I'm used to it by now," Jacob replied.

"Your life must be messed up if this is normal to you," Cloe said, feeling a little sad for Jacob.

"No, it's not that bad. With power comes great responsibility; I like to think that this is our duty for being blessed with these amazing powers" Jacob said.

"Well, when you put it like that it doesn't sound so bad. So what are we going to do now?" Cloe asked.

"I don't know, but did you see what happened to them? I think when I and Amelia closed the gate on Halloween that must have ticked him off," Jacob said.

"Yeah like, really royally. So, what is the new plan, Jacob? Where should we look next?" Cloe asked.

"I don't know. Maybe we could try looking in the Mirror Dimension for him," Jacob said.

"Well okay, but don't you remember how dangerous it is in there from when we were younger?"

"Yes, I know, but we have to find him: so will you come?" Jacob asked.

Cloe took a moment to think about her answer; she had never gone on these dangerous missions before, and she was not sure what to expect. However, she agreed to go because if they didn't find Half Penny the whole town of dark woods would be filled with a massacre of dead bodies. So they decided to enter the darkness of the mirror dimension again. They packed up their supplies; Journal#1, a camera and an ancient whistle called "the whistle of Raxaer" which was used to make evil spirits disappear. Later on, that night at the stroke of midnight when the moon was in place of the sky the moon began to turn green. Jacob and Cloe channelled all of their powers and opened a portal to the Mirror Dimension, and then they jumped through the gateway and landed in the mirror dimension version of his house in the forest.

The mirror dimension was more terrifying than Cloe had imagined; perhaps it was the illusion of a real world that Cloe knew perfectly well didn't exist. Also, she knew they could run into all manner of creatures in here and this scared her. She could also not shake off the feeling that they were being watched. The timelines between day and night were different in the mirror dimension. It could get dark at any time and light could come at any time too. There was also a misty appearance about the place, making it hard to see more than a hundred yards ahead. Also, it seemed to be dawn or dusk even when it was daytime. It was getting darker and darker right now, so Jacob created purple and black flames for some light with his hands and eyes. Cloe created red and black flames too to guide them. They began to hear swirling and crawling sounds and as they looked in the city hall version, they saw decapitated dead rotting bodies all over. The stench was so horrible that it made Cloe want to throw up. The bodies were bent in every direction, and some were missing hands, legs, eyes, and even heads! It was truly a terrible sight to behold.

Cloe felt she had stepped on some branches and so she looked down. It was at this point that she noticed that their feet were covered with black vines with ghostly blue light glowing out of them.

"Oh my goodness; what are these, Jacob?" Cloe asked panicking.

"Don't move, Cloe; first let me confirm if they are a threat," Jacob cautioned her.

Chapter 5

POSSESSED

Jacob got Journal#1 out and read the vines' profile page: it said that in the mirror dimension these were the devil's plants and should not be messed with. The vines were capable of choking someone to death when disturbed. They would wrap themselves around their victims and squeeze the life out of them. The journal advised that to escape them one should not make any quick or slow movements. It also warned them that if they grabbed you, they would never let go.

"That is so creepy! So how are we going to escape the tower if we can't move?" Cloe wondered tensely.

"I don't know – resort to flight or go invincible maybe…I don't know. The journal says the vines have two weaknesses: heat, fire and weed killer but if we use fire, it could attract unwanted attention," Jacob said.

"I have not mastered the invincible spell yet," Cloe said. "Perhaps we could just teleport to escape maybe?"

"Yeah, let's do it," Jacob agreed.

They teleported away to the cabin of horror that Eliot and Tom had been to last Halloween. They noticed the strange dolls and somehow Jacob recognized the dolls from last Halloween. They also noticed the red and blue lights as they entered the basement; it made the place look very creepy and gave Jacob a very bad feeling, but they walked on. At that moment, they realised they were walking on the vines, aka the devil's plants, but this time they realised it was too late. The vines captured both Jacob and Cloe by wrapping themselves around their bodies. The grip was so tight that the two could not even wiggle out of it. Cloe felt as if it was squeezing the air out of her body. The light began to blink off and on while making thunder sounds and glowing green. Jacob understood these signs very well: Half Penny was here. He felt a cold chill run down his spine as he prepared himself for the worst.

"Well, well, well, look what we have here. This is such a pleasant surprise!" Half Penny said, giggling. "We are going to have so much fun together."

There he was, looking like a puppet but with the most terrifying face Cloe had ever seen and fingers that looked like claws. But the scariest thing was the intense evil in his fiery eyes.

"You know we are not here by choice. If you are so confident in yourself release us from these vines so you can play fair," Jacob challenged him.

"Now why would I ever do that? Who cares about playing fair? Certainly not me. Oh, and I see you've met an old friend. This is going to be so much fun," Half Penny said before breaking into a peal of evil laughter.

"Let us go, Half Penny", Cloe cried out.

"Oh, it speaks!" Half penny said, mocking Cloe. "Well, if you know my name then you know I don't abide by the requests of little kids. Now what to do about you little kids, huh? Oh, I know. Possession!"

Jacob and Cloe cried out in protest, but it was already too late. Everything happened so fast. In a flash, half penny had possessed both

Cloe and Jacob. His first mission was to channel their powers to escape the Mirror Dimension and now he found himself in the woods of Dark Woods. He was so pleased with himself that he started laughing out loud.

"I didn't know I could have even done something like that before!" Half Penny said to himself in a distorted voice. "I am going to have so much fun in these new bodies! As the darkness rises my power grows, so I guess I'll have to get the books myself."

Cloe - under Half Penny's possession - walked to Dark Woods to get revenge on everyone who was a part of ruining his Halloween last year. Jacob too was possessed by Half Penny and was on a mission to do his bidding. Half Penny first directed him to go to Jenny Clark's apartment. The woman was sound asleep in his bedroom with the lights still on. The poor woman was afraid of the dark after all the strange happenings at Dark Woods. As much as she was fast asleep, she was a light sleeper and was always aware if someone was in the room, so when she felt a shadow cast over her body, she woke up in terror. She let out a scream when she saw Jacob standing over her body with a wicked grin on his face.

"What...what are you doing here and how did you get in?" Jenny Clark screamed.

"Hush...so you don't remember me?" Half Penny said, grinning.

"You're the boy at school from four weeks ago," Jenny said, racking her brains.

"Well, technically yes...but this is not my body...keep guessing," Jacob prompted.

Jenny was so confused. "What was this little boy going on about at this ungodly hour?" she wondered to herself. She was too tired of all this back and forth, so she decided to play his game.

"Okay, I don't know who you are, please tell me," Jenny Clark said.

"Seems you can't remember me, but I know who you are. I'm the one who caused what happened to you last Halloween," Jacob said with a wicked grin.

Jenny gasped in shock; she had a traumatic flashback of seeing Half Penny in the mirror dimension from last Halloween. She crouched further away in her bed from the possessed Jacob. She had had nightmares of this creature and now he had followed her to her home.

"Oh my God, you are the puppet from that dark place," Jenny whimpered.

"Yes honey, and oh, if you tell anyone about me –I will come back and kill you for real this time. I have left something behind your bedroom curtain. I'll come for it when I'm ready," he threatened her before disappearing, laughing in hi sinister spine-chilling way.

Jenny Clark was terrified when Half Penny had gone. What had he left behind the curtain? She was both curious and terrified. Unable to sleep after that, she switched on the light and crept towards the curtain. Then something moved and fell on to the floor, and she realized it was a skull. She screamed and fell on her back. Then a hand that seemed like Half Penny's reached in through the window and grabbed the skull and was gone, again with that eerie laughter.

Jenny was too terrified to speak. She sat there hyperventilating and sweating, she couldn't believe that had just happened. She was too scared to go back to sleep, so she lay awake until morning.

Early that morning, possessed Jacob and Cloe were walking aimlessly through without any proper direction. They were walking through a dangerous wooded area where kids were known to be kidnapped and killed on their way to school. Suddenly, two men wearing ski masks came out of the woods and grabbed them and took them to the back of a van. They took them to a warehouse and chained them up to a chair. That is when the brutal beatings began as the guys demanded they give them everything they possessed. Both Jacob and Cloe just sat there taking in the beatings but not feeling a damn thing, after all – they were possessed.

"Who in their stupid minds kidnaps kids and hopes to get something valuable from them? Are you this dumb?" Jacob mocked them.

"Shut up you little idiot; you are in no position to talk," one of the men slapped him across the face, his face flashing with a murderous light.

"You guys have no idea what a stupid mistake you have just made kidnapping us," possessed Cloe said, laughing. Jacob joined in on the laughter.

The murderers were taken aback by the bravery of these two kids. The kids they normally kidnapped would be weeping and peeing on themselves at this point but these two were mocking them and laughing!

"So what are you going to do?" one of the murderers challenged them while pointing a gun at their heads.

"Oh, you are about to find out," Jacob replied, smirking.

At that very moment, Jacob and Cloe broke out of his chain very easily and the chains fell to the floor. Jacob turned into a purple electrical storm in the shape of a demon and possessed Cloe turned into a red electrical storm in the shape of a demon. The murderers screamed in terror while the two demon-possessed people brutally burned them alive in hot flames. The heat that radiated outwards consumed everything until there were only ashes. One could hear the crackling of their charred bodies and the pungent smell of burnt hair. The flickering sparks flew around the room and dropped one by one on the floor. The thick smoke that emanated was enough to choke someone to death, but thankfully Jacob and Cloe at this point were no human.

They flew out of the window back to the woods of Dark Woods.

Chapter 6

A CASE LIKE NO OTHER

Meanwhile the police, accompanied by the ambulance, arrived at the warehouse. On alighting from their vehicles, their mouths went agape as they stood stupefied by the scene. One police officer was so sickened by the horrifying scene and couldn't stand the sight of blood and threw up uncontrollably. One of the paramedics from the ambulance lost consciousness as the rest stood shaking their heads sadly. They couldn't believe that they were too late to save lives. The police constable with them couldn't quite decipher what had transpired. In his mind, he kept getting flashbacks from last Halloween. He had been part of the team that was investigating the murder at the house in the woods last year. The recent unfolding in the news left him wondering if there was a possibility that they could be dealing with the same perpetrator. Most members from the team that had responded that day were coincidentally in the previous response team. The same thought of dealing with the creepy happening of the previous Halloween lingered in their thoughts and they were terrified by the death full massacre, and it was more horrifying than they could have imagined. With the intent to bring the perpetrator to book, the team's first thought was to contact a detective named Detective Cyrus Sinan to investigate the strange and supernatural deaths going on in Dark Woods and find an answer to it. This was because they believed that

Det Sinan was very good at what he did. He was famed for unravelling some of the most mysterious and baffling crime scenes in Dark Woods. He had been nick-named 'the stone turner' as he never left any stone unturned. The detective gladly accepted the request and availed himself almost immediately at the crime scene. Solving crimes was his best hobby and he couldn't help getting excited to get to the bottom of the whole scene. This was however a very big mistake, and he was putting himself in great danger. He was trying to attempt finding a perpetrator whose hands were itchy for blood. One whose main goal was to bring fear, terror and tears into anyone that tried crossing his path! The police and paramedics looked at him sadly as he walked into the house to start off his investigation. They thought that this was probably the last day they would see the detective alive. They were too spooked to offer to accompany him inside the house, so they dawdled outside, awaiting further instructions. As the detective reached for the door handle and made to open it, his spectators covered their eyes as they feared that the detective was just giving death a piggy-back ride. As the door creaked open, the driver of the ambulance unknowingly grabbed the emergency response doctor's hand and clung onto it as he trembled as a feeble branch. As for the police, they all cowered into their van except for the constable who, though very shaken, stood his ground with his weapon drawn in anticipation to fire. The house was very dark, and the detective could barely see anything even with his flashlight. As he kept walking further inside, he thought he had heard something, and he turned swiftly to see what it was. His flashlight flickered and as he peered into the darkness, he shivered a little. He was always against Halloween pranks, but this seemed like an entirely different story. The pranks were just pranks but this was a completely different scenario. There were real dead bodies on the floor and the whole scene was horrifying. He turned to make another step into the dark house, and he heard a chuckle from one side. He shook off the thought and assumed that it was because he had let the Halloween thoughts get into his mind. He kept walking cautiously with an intention to unravel the mystery. Then the chuckle came again; a more distinct and audible one this time. Detective Sinan trembled a little and as he turned around his flashlight fell on the floor and went off. The chuckle turned into an evil laughter as a thunderous slap landed on his left cheek, then he felt his ears being pulled as the laughter got louder by the second. He felt a hand grab his and he screamed in horror as he galloped out of the house as soon as he untangled himself from the grip. When he got outside, he found the whole group cowed together, all struggling to be in the middle. The detective was shaken as he had never seen such a thing before. He stood in a daze as he pondered his next move. He was on the verge of throwing in the towel, but his zest to unravel the mystery got the better part of him. After a long spell of silence, each drowning in their own thoughts as they trembled, Detective Sinan called out to them.

"Hey guys, listen up. Since it is getting dark, I suggest that we get some back up lights and some police to stand guard then we shall resume the investigation tomorrow morning."

"What happened, detective?" one nurse asked. "We heard some screams."

The detective looked at the nurse for a minute or two then looked down. He seemed disappointed with himself.

"I really don't know what happened in there but there is more than meets the eye. I felt something I cannot explain grab my hand. It was

36

as if someone was trying to mock me, and it was all dark. I got spooked as I thought this was just another normal case, but I was mistaken. It is no ordinary case," he said as he paced up and down while speaking his thoughts.

The rest of the team was dumbfounded as they didn't expect such utterance from the brave detective.

"Oh, wait! How about we check it out right now then we can start the investigation tomorrow?" the detective suggested. The team stared at him without a word. "C'mon guys, we each have a flashlight. Besides, once we satisfy our curiosity, we will be able to sleep well tonight," he insisted. One by one, the team shook their heads as they took a number of steps further from the warehouse and without a word, they boarded their cars. The detective, on seeing this, hurried to his car and drove off. He didn't want to be left in the scary place all by himself. He made sure that he wasn't the last to leave, he eventually found himself leading the convoy from the warehouse and he laughed to himself that he was never going back to that place. Little did he know that his entry into the warehouse had already been noticed by Half Penny!

Meanwhile in the forest of Dark Woods Lucy and her friends Sera, Luna, Jenny and there new friend Sam were walking to Robin Good's house to talk to him and asked him to come with them to the city hall to see if there was a clue to whatever evil was out there, but when he was about to decline they mentioned that Half Penny was out of his book and he agreed to join them on their quest. As they were walking through the woods running from what they thought was a person they fell through a trap door and found themselves in the sewers beneath the city hall and saw that toxins and discovered that whatever magic curse Half Penny was using on last Halloween night has been turned into ashes of some kind of book. That got Lucy thinking about the time last year when Tom and Eliot mentioned that they found a dead man with a page in his cold hands and that got them the idea that there might be someone or something in Dark Woods who was being possessed by Half Penny and he had come back to finish what he started last Halloween. Jenny, however, was more concerned that if Half Penny found out what she was doing he would brutally come back to kill her.

Chapter 7

MORE THAN THE POLICE CAN HANDLE

Later on, that day in the house where Tom and Eliot found the Horror Halloween book, Detective Cyrus Sinan and Chief Officer Johnathan Raven were investigating the creepy house. They had called two of the neighbours in case they needed to ask a question or two, and they also had three constables with them. Boards placed against the windows where curtains had once been made the rooms very dark, and the electricity had long been disconnected, so that anyone going in required a flashlight. As they made their way to the room where the Horror Halloween book was hidden away before Tom and Eliot found it last year, the detectives felt a little shaken. Detective Sinan still felt a little shaken by the previous ordeal. The thought of the ordeal repeating itself made him shudder. He however knew that he had to shake it off as he was leading the investigation. Somewhere deep down he was curious to get behind the strange happenings around Halloween. The rest of the group walked in silence, each lost in their own thoughts. Some of them walked as a huddle as they were in complete fear.

"C'mon! Don't be cowards," Detective Sinan challenged as he broke into a short nervous laughter. The group smiled in an effort to put on a brave face in the midst of what seemed like weird unexplained mystery – something they had had to contend with since the Halloween mystery; a series of strange events happening around Dark Woods that had the best detectives on the force totally baffled. In a cowardly way they approached the door to the room. Somewhere along the corridor, quite close to the room, they all seemed to come to a halt, maybe contemplating the next move. The detective could have sworn that some of those with him were considering the option of turning back. He too wasn't too sure about going into the room, and he slowed his walk and looked back at the group.

"Does everyone have a flashlight?" he asked as he tried to make himself brave. They all nodded in agreement as he urged them to get closer to him.

"Keep close to each other. Make sure you know every officer who is here and who is next to you, and you can account for them once we are in there," he said as he nodded towards the room. He turned his head to look at his group. Some of them were visibly shaking and this made the lead detective even more worried about tagging them along into the room for the investigation of the scene.

"I know that some of you are scared by the media frenzy about supernatural events. But we must think in a rational way as officers…," he started. "The important thing to remember is that we are here to investigate the incident in this room, and it is very important to remain close to each other. Grab hold of your partner's hand if you have to. I cannot let you turn back at this spot as it is very risky for you to be out there on your own. So we are in this together. Everyone, turn your flashlight on and come with me. Anyone with something to say?" he asked. They all shook their heads, but they did not dare say a word.

"Come on! Let's go!" the detective said as he made a step towards the room. With every sound magnified in the dark, somehow his feet seemed to have been glued onto the floor as he seemed stuck at the same spot. He however gathered courage as he still wanted to get to know what was on the other side of the door in the room. As he made a couple of more steps, his group seemed huddled together as they didn't make a move. He stopped as though to wait for them to get to where he was. So many thoughts were running through his head as he wondered if he really was doing the right thing. He still couldn't believe that he had gladly accepted the challenge of working on this case. He had worked so many weird crime cases but so far, this was not a normal case as he had come to learn. It was nothing compared to what he had worked on previously. There seemed to have some mystical happenings propagated by some supernatural force. He at some point almost regretted taking up the job.

He was completely lost in thought when something happened, that made his heart skip a beat. He felt a hand on his shoulder! He could not even turn around. In his mind, he was very sure that the happenings from before were repeating himself and he shook a little.

"Easy, man. Let's go," said Jonathan Raven as he nudged him gently to hold the door knob. Detective Sinan was a little relieved.

"Phew! It's you. Why did you sneak up on me like that? I almost thought the ghost was onto me," he said nervously as he looked at the other officers with him. Most of them feigned a smile that looked so ludicrous that Detective Sinan almost burst into laughter. Their faces were plastered with the fear of the surrounding then masked up with a fake smile! Detective Sinan shook his head and went for the door knob.

As he turned the door knob, he could have sworn that some of the members of his group took a step or two backwards while others stared intently at the door in a bid to satisfy their curiosity. As the door creaked open, the silence was so loud that you could hear a pin drop. They all held their breath as they peered into the dark room. No one dared to make a step into the room, so they stood at the door. Detective Sinan knew that he had to be a little brave, so he made a step and beckoned the rest to follow him. They shuffled timidly into the room. While at least Tom, Eliot and the others were dealing with a known enemy, the detectives were dealing with something they did not know.

"Remember what I told you? Be attentive to any detail as it might help unravel this case. Make sure that you stay close to each other. I would hate it if I lost anyone during this process. Okay?" Detective Cyrus asked. They all nodded in agreement of some sort. They were barely listening to Detective Cyrus as they kept looking all around them as though they were expecting an ambush any time.

"Alright! Let's get to work then." The detective said as he made another step into the darkness. The light from his flashlight flickered him a little but he felt braver now that he knew he was not alone. He had his group who almost acted as spectators.

Detective Cyrus asked: "Has anyone lived in this house since the murder of 2015?" the people shrugged.

"Are you crazy?" Jonathan Raven asked. "Everybody in dark woods thinks this place is haunted!" he continued to say.

Detective Cyrus stared at him for a moment then said, "Well, everyone seems to be probably right. Actually, after what happened last Halloween, I do not think this is a coincidence. In my opinion, I think something very dangerous is coming, Jonathan. Something pure dark and evil." Everyone seemed scared. They looked at each other with horror written all over their faces.

Then Jonathan Raven asked, "So what should we do about it? You know if it were up to me, I think we should tell Sergeant Wilson, Rick Alder and Collins to come and look with us. What do you think about that?"

Detective Cyrus exclaimed, "No! It has happened once today, so I have the suspicion that it will happen very, very soon today, so I'm gonna wait. So we must stay here and tell them to keep our and their mouths shut and our ears and eyes open!"

Johnathan Raven then asked, "Okay so where do you think it will happen next?"

Detective Cyrus seemed to ignore the question as he looked around the room without making any step. He then felt his hair stand on end and a chill ran up his spine as that laughter came again. Then the door behind them slammed shut, and there was the sound of wind blowing inside the house, like a strong gale. Detective Sinan had just discovered a knob that belonged to a drawer under the curtain. It seemed that the drawers were inside the wall under the window. But as the board that covered the window began to move in wards as if a hand was pushing it, he hesitated and heard that laughter again.

The two neighbours were the first to run out of the room, and soon Det Sinan was alone. He followed them outside. Whatever it was he felt he couldn't handle it alone. As he rushed out of the house after the others, he glanced back and saw that the house was flooded with a bluish light.

Chapter 8

HOME ALONE

Meanwhile in the tower where the portal was closed possessed Jacob and Cloe were standing in the basement and had brought a whole mini army of living demon voodoo dolls to life with their magic and Half Penny became happy that he was back, and he was going after his next target Amelia and Jack that night. He was happy that he had discouraged the detectives from investigating the house without revealing himself to them. Later on that dark night at the Normans' house Jack and Amelia were home alone and were playing chess while their parents were out. They were in the middle of a game when the lights began to blink off and on while glowing green and making thunder sounds. The two were a little scared, then they thought that there would be a downpour. The thought of Half Penny attacking them never crossed their minds. They however couldn't account for the flickering of the lights.

"What's going on?" Amelia asked Jack. Jack shrugged his shoulders.

"I think there's going to be a power outage. It happens at times when there is a heavy downpour. I read it somewhere that the power company switches off the power to reduce the damage from lightning and thunder," Jack said. Amelia seemed not to buy his statement and she looked at him with a raised eyebrow.

"Well, I don't know how true it is. I mean, it was just a theory to account for the constant power outages when it rains," Jack said.

"Well, alright then. You haven't made a move yet," she said. Jack put his thumb, index finger and middle finger on the 'Bishop' and made as if he was picking it up to make a move. Then he thought he had heard a voice and he paused, then went on to make his move.

"Ha! Ha! Ha!" came loud thunderous laughter. "Wrong move!" the voice continued to boom.

"Did you hear that?" Amelia asked Jack.

"Yes, I heard it, Amelia. Look you don't have to mock me. I am still learning chess. I am not a pro as you are!" Jack exclaimed angrily.

"But Jack, I didn't say a word. Wait a minute, have you ever heard me talk that loudly? I cannot even laugh that loudly," Amelia explained.

"Mm…so who said that? It's just the two of us here," Jack observed.

He had barely finished talking when a shadowy dark figure appeared and began messing with their chess board.

"Quit it, Jack! It's not funny!" Amelia shouted angrily.

"What do you mean?" Jack asked.

"Oh, quit pretending. Stop messing with the board."

"But I didn't do anything, Amelia," Jack said.

All this while, the dark shadowy figure was hovering over Jack, but Amelia barely noticed it as the lights were still flickering. For a moment, the lights went completely dark and when they came back on, and Amelia felt a resounding slap on her cheek. She thought that Jack had slapped her and made as if to slap him too, then stopped mid-action when he saw Jack struggling to pull back as though something was pulling him away from the table. On seeing this, Amelia was thrown into a daze. She didn't know what to do and stood motionless as she watched helplessly as Jack screamed for help.

45

When she came to her senses, she ran towards Jack to help him, but before she reached where he was, she slid and fell on her back. For a moment things seemed a little blurry as her head had been seriously hit. She could hear Jack's screams, but they seemed to be coming from far away. For a moment everything went dark. Then before long, she regained her consciousness. It was then that she saw Jack on the floor, his eyes wide open. There was terror written all over his face. He was shaking like a twig. He tried to stretch his hand to reach Amelia, but his hand was not strong. The two lay there for a moment, both stupefied by the ordeal. Before long, there were more thunderous chuckles and a commotion. Amelia and Jack had by now managed to crawl towards each other and they cuddled in fear as they shuddered at the thought of what could happen next. Suddenly they heard the door slamming. After a few seconds it creaked wide open. None of them dared to move.

"Come on you cowards! Let's dance!" the voice boomed mockingly at them. They still did not move. The lights started flickering again with ghostly images surrounding them. All this while, echoes of thunderous laughter were being heard all over the house. This made the children even more scared! Amelia couldn't even hold back, and she broke down into tears as Jack looked at her helplessly. He did not know what to do. The scare he had suffered moments ago was still quite fresh in his mind. He could not quite decipher what was pulling him nor where he was being pulled into! He had barely recovered when he heard a gentle howl, then something touched his leg. He leapt up at a surprising speed, but not before he heard a mocking laughter. He couldn't really make out where the laughter was emanating from. He yelped and screamed in fear.

46

"Hello, who's there?" he asked. "Amelia?" he called out as he gasped for air. It was pitch black in the house and he could not see a thing.

Then Jacob responded in a dark and distorted voice, "It is an old friend, Jack and Amelia. Don't you remember me?" He chuckled.

"Who is this? Amelia asked in a weak and shaken voice.

"Who is this?" Jacob mimicked and mocked Amelia in a dark and distorted voice.

Then Amelia asked, "Are you the one who killed the people at the warehouse earlier today?"

Possessed Jacob replied, "Yes I am." Amelia trembled a little and as she shot her electrical blast at the shadowy figure it was revealed to be Jacob.

"Jacob?" Amelia called out. "Is that you?" she asked. Unknown to them however was that he wasn't alone, and he was still possessed by Half Penny.

"What are you doing here?" Jack asked curiously as he stared at Jacob.

"I'm here to have what you have; the books!" he responded to them darkly. It was as if the voice was a combination of both Jacob and Half Penny, and this made it very creepy. Amelia felt a little concerned. Jacob was never one to talk in this way. She however did not mention a thing to Jack.

Jacob kept staring at them emotionlessly, awaiting a response. As he began to attack them Amelia began to fight back and before she could attack Jacob, he turned invisible to avoid being killed.

"Where are you? Show yourself!" Jack challenged. "Amelia, maybe we should call the others, don't you think?" he suggested.

Amelia replied: "It's just one monster; I'm pretty sure we can take it."

When Possessed Jacob heard this, he growled impatiently, and then said in a dark and distorted voice: "Don't be so sure!"

Though they were scared that their friend Jacob was turning on them, they were enraged at the thought that their friend had betrayed them. As they walked slowly around the house voodoo dolls began attacking them one at a time, but the two kids started to look inside the house and as they went up to the attic they were suddenly attacked by Cloe, who unknown to them had powers like Amelia. As she was fighting Cloe, she was shocked to see that she had powers like her too and as Jack shot a stone right at Cloe's face with his slingshot and she was knocked to the ground, the lights began to turn off and on while making thunder sounds and glowing green. Both Jack and Amelia began to shake and were scared about what was about to happen to them that night of dark and pure evil. Meanwhile had left the creepy house and had just received the report that there were bangs and lights blinking off at the Normans' house. As both Possessed Jacob and Cloe began to brutally attack Jack and Amelia, this time they were using the puppet army. As the puppets pinned Amelia and Jack to the ground, Amelia went into a rage and released a huge electrical blast and made the puppets, Possessed Jacob and Cloe crash to the walls. As Amelia and Jack had both Possessed Jacob and Cloe cornered to the attic walls, they realized that they appeared to be dead. When they touched their necks, they noticed that they seemed to have no pulse and assumed they were dead.

It was then they heard a knock on the door downstairs. Amelia and Jack glanced at each other. Were their parents back or had some neighbours noticed or heard the strange happenings inside the house? When they glanced back towards the wall, they noticed that Jacob and Cloe had disappeared!

The doorbell rang again. Amelia and Jack looked at each other again as they took off to open the door. They found Detective Cyrus standing outside and were a little relieved to see him. Since he was in plain clothes, they did not know that he was a police officer. Detective Cyrus was shocked to see the state they were in. Jack had a swollen eye that seemed to be bleeding and his face seemed well battered and red. His lower lip had a deep cut that seemed to ooze blood, and his clothes seemed all tattered and bloody. His head was clean shaven on one side. His neck had some visible claw marks.

Amelia's appearance shocked the detective even more. Her face had what seemed like bites from a human being. Her eyes were red, lips swollen with a deep cut on the lower one, her hair seemed to have been glued together and shaped to resemble two horns like that of a goat! Her clothes had been torn as though someone was working on them with a pair of scissors. A keen look in between the rips showed that there was a visible deep cut on the left leg that gushed blood continuously. The two kids appeared ghostly.

"What's going on here, kids? I heard all sorts of noises. I also found one of your neighbours at the gate and she says she heard them too."

"It's really nothing," Jack said, trying to avoid having to explain about Half Penny as they had always done. What could they say? The man would not believe that they had seen a weird creature that resembled a clawed puppet, and Half Penny would probably not reveal himself to adults – up until now he seemed not to reveal himself to anyone but

Jacob and Jacob's close friends. Jack and Amelia did not know that the detective was already investigating the Half Penny case.

"Well, I'll have to find out for myself. Where are your parents? I can see from the state you are in that something happened. Have you two been fighting?"

"No," Amelia said. She tried to hit him with a blast to keep away, but she did not want him to know that she had these powers, so she stopped.

Chapter 9

HALLUCINATIONS

As they invited Detective Cyrus into the house, the detective could see them limping painfully. Inside the house, the scenery made the detective open his mouth in bewilderment. The living room seemed as though it had been hit by a tornado. The seats were all upside down, and the cooking pans in the kitchen were scattered all over the place. A couple of knives were dangling dangerously from the ceiling, threatening to drop any moment. The TV was on the floor and broken porcelain was all over. There was a mop on the floor that he almost tripped on as he walked into the house. The stairs and the passage that led to the rest of the rooms was filled with clothes, water, forks and broken glass. He stood there for some time trying to take in what he had just seen. This was way too much! He thought the kids appeared to be well behaved children. He couldn't quite comprehend what had transpired there. The place plus the children were in a complete mess. He was now more convinced that some other power was at play in all this!

When he finally found his voice and words, he began questioning them about what had happened to them that night of horror.

"Oh my! What the hell happened here?" he asked. The kids stared at him blankly.

"And who might you be?" Jack asked. It was a sort of formality as they didn't expect him there at that time of the night.

Detective Cyrus raised his eyebrows. "Well, I am detective Cyrus, and I am investigating the supernatural deaths and strange unexplained events in Dark Woods that have happened here since last Halloween."

Amelia said, "Well, we don't know … we thought we just saw a living puppet, but it was probably just an hallucination."

Detective Cyrus eyebrows rose a little. "Are you sure?"

"Well, maybe. I don't know," said Jack, avoiding eye contact with the detective.

"What happened to you guys?"

"Nothing much really sir," Jack said.

"Hmmm … nothing much? Wow, that's the understatement of the year!" the detective exclaimed. "Come on, you can do better than this." The detective pressed for more information.

The kids just looked at each other and shrugged. "There is really nothing much to say about it sir," Amelia said.

"You know you can talk to me. In case I didn't mention, I am a detective. So, if you were attacked, I will gladly look for the perpetrators and bring them to book. So, tell me. What happened?" Detective Cyrus asked.

Amelia looked at Jack's face then said, "It was just some sort of hallucination that made us cause this mess, sir. We are sorry but that is really what happened."

The detective nodded and said, "Alright then. If you find anything suspicious don't hesitate to give me a call. Okay? Have a good night." Then he seemed to change his mind. He wasn't convinced with the kids' story and vowed to himself that he would keep a keen eye on them.

In an effort to make him leave, Amelia secretly threw a microscopic blast at him. He placed his hand on his chest and groaned. "Suddenly I don't feel so well."

He decided to investigate the house and they didn't stop him, but all he found in the attic was just a voodoo puppet. He wrote something down, wrote down their home address and left.

The next morning as Jack and Amelia were walking down the street on their way to the Tuckers' house to warn the others about what has happened to them last night, but as they walked, they had the suspicion that they were being watched. At that moment as they were running Jack's head began to hurt worse than a migraine and he had a vision. It was as if he could sense Half Penny hanging around. They rushed to the Ticker house.

Amelia yelled: "Hello Tom, Eliot; open the door!" as she rang and knocked on the front door.

When the front door opened Tom and Eliot began asking what was wrong, Jack and Amelia then rushed them urgently to the treehouse very quickly because Tom and Eliot's folks were home and might overhear. Once they arrived, they asked where Luna and Lucy were. Luna had become Lucy's very close friend and often visited the Tickers to hang out with Lucy, Tom and Eliot.

Eliot replied, "Oh, well … they went to investigate if anything was happening at the sewers in the city hall tower."

Amelia and Jack explained that Jacob had gone totally rogue and had tried to kill them both and had the help of a girl named Cloe who had power too. Tom and Eliot were shocked to realize that four people now had powers so far, and that they now had a new adversary named Detective Cyrus who was onto them and who might know about Half

53

Penny and about the journals. So they decided that first they needed to stop Jacob and stop Detective Cyrus from finding out the truth about what had happened. If he found out he would be able to link Jacob's journals to Jacob and to all of them and they may be blamed for working with Half Penny or hiding information from the police.

Eliot asked, "So, what should we do about Jacob?"

"Well, maybe we should go find the others, coz we are going to need all the help we can get to stop two people with dark magic powers," Jack replied. "What do you suggest we do, Tom?" he asked as he looked at Tom.

"Hmmm, yeah, me too; I agree," he said. "So should we go now?" he added.

"Okay, let's go," Amelia said.

As Amelia, Eliot, Tom and Jack were walking through the city hall building trying to find them, Eliot decided to give Lucy a call on his phone, but she didn't answer.

"Guys, I think we have a problem," he said. Amelia, Tom and Jack stopped in their tracks to listen to Eliot.

"What do you mean?" Amelia asked.

"What kind of problem?" Tom chimed in.

"It's Lucy," he said.

"What about her?" asked Jack.

"She is not picking my call, which is odd because she always has her phone with her and never misses a phone call."

"For how long has she not picked your call?" Tom asked inquisitively.

"A few minutes ago," Eliot said while looking down at the ground with a thoughtful frown.

"It is too early to raise an alarm. Give her some more time to see if she will call you back. Maybe she is having a nap," Amelia suggested.

When Tom noticed that he was having problems with his phone network as well, he suggested that maybe whatever machines were in the tower were messing with the signal, and at that moment when Jack was leaning against the wall, he opened a secret room full of ancient technology dating back to an unknown date. They had never seen these devices before. They seemed very old; from a bygone era many centuries ago, and yet they seemed very sophisticated.

"What is that? Looks like a rectangular clock and it's still ticking. I've never seen anything like that," Jack said, pointing at what looked like a silver clock covered with dust. It looked like it had stood here for a long, long time.

"Look, it has days, months, years and right now it's showing today's date. And it has a door – and look, enough room for somebody to step into it."

"Maybe it's a time machine," Eliot said, and they laughed.

"Only one way to find out," Tom said. "Step inside and we'll turn the dial to a different year, and you'll see if you'll go back to that time, Jack."

"Who, me?" Jack gaped.

"Come on, don't say you are scared!" Eliot said scornfully. "I would happily do it myself, but somebody has to monitor and control the time machine for the sake of the person in the machine in case it's really a time machine!"

"What? Are you saying that my life will be in danger when I'm in that contraption? Because if that's the case, there is no way I'm getting in!" Jack said heatedly.

"I don't think it's a time machine," Tom said. "I'll step inside if Jack's too scared."

Jack opened the glass door and Seth reluctantly got in. "I feel groggy," he complained.

Amelia grabbed a bottle standing on a shelf and opened it. "What's this? Smells like a fruit drink."

She took a sip. Hiding in the shadows, Half Penny grinned. He knew that he had messed with that drink and had impressed upon her mind to take that sip. Causing hallucinations was one of his new tricks.

"Don't drink that, you idiot!" Tom yelled. "It could have been here for years!"

Amelia swayed and staggered. "Did you see that, Uncle? The time machine spun twice."

"No it didn't. Maybe the stuff you drank is already taking effect," Eliot said worriedly. He wanted to turn the dial on the 'time machine' but Amelia was behaving very strangely, and they turned their attention on her.

"Watch out, Tom!" Amelia cried, pointing at Eliot. "I think he wants to kill you."

"Tom, go with her outside. I don't know what she drank but she's hallucinating. I'll see if this time machine works."

"Will you promise not to kill me?" Amelia asked Tom as he tried to push her towards the door. Her eyes seemed dazed, and she could hardly stand.

"I promise," Tom said.

"Something is wrong," Amelia said as they left. "Eliot wants to commit a murder and wants us out of the room before he does."

Tom laughed.

Eliot turned to Jack. "Can you hear me, Jack?"

"Yes, but I feel very sleepy," Jack said, his speech slurred.

"I'm about to turn the dial so we can see if it works. Now, what point in history do you want to revisit?"

"Ancient Egypt," Jack said, dragging his words and his lips hardly moving.

"Hmmm...interesting. Shall we say...51 B.C. then. Interesting characters back then."

*

"What is that at the window?" Amelia shouted as soon as they were inside another room. "Do you see it? It's a shadow...no, it's Half Penny! No, it's Jacob!"

"Where? Which is which? Is it Half Penny or Jacob?"

"I can't tell," Amelia stumbled again. She tried to focus on the image of Half Penny outside the window, but she couldn't. Whatever she had drank made her dizzy and she almost fell, but Tom grabbed her before she could.

Amelia was not sure what was happening, but everything was so real. Now she was in the living room back home. The living room door swung open, and two men dressed in ski masks came in.

Now she saw that it was Half Penny in a ski mask. He held a giant clock in his hands, just like the one Jack had stepped into in the other room. Then Amelia saw that it was ticking.

"It's a bomb!" she exclaimed. She pointed at the. "It's a bomb! We are going to die! Come on, Tom...." She grabbed Tom's hand.

Half Penny laughed his sinister laugh, but Amelia was not sure if she was hallucinating or if he was really there.

"A bomb? Where?" Tom looked around frantically. "I don't see it. You are hallucinating, Amelia."

"I'm not!" Amelia yelled angrily.

"What's going on?" Eliot had come to the next room when he heard them shouting.

"She says she can see Half Penny and Jacob too and Half Penny has a bomb."

"Must be that drink," Eliot said.

"But what if it's real?" Tom insisted.

Amelia suddenly stretched out her hands towards the window and a blur flame shot out, but this seemed to take all her energy away and she was about to crash head first on to the concrete when Eliot grabbed her and placed her gently on the floor.

"Let her lie there for now," he said. "Let's see if Tom has anything to report. He said he wants to try 51 BC. Maybe he's learnt interesting stuff in his history lessons."

So they stepped back into the room with ancient devices.

Chapter 10

TIME TRAVEL

J ack was acutely aware that all eyes were painfully riveted on him, and the room was so quiet you could have heard a pin drop. He was just as he had been dressed when he entered the time machine, but he did not recall anything to do with a time machine. All he recalled was being in the room with Tom, Eliot and Amelia. He had been wearing an orange T-shirt and blue jeans and sneakers. He had a watch on, his phone was in his pocket.

Jack was standing in an ancient hall full of amazing things that looked very expensive. In front of him was a woman seated, with a crown on her head. Several women and armed men stood behind her.

"Who are you? Your clothes are strange indeed," the queen said. "I am Queen Cleopatra, and you shall call me Your Highness, stranger."

Jack decided he had better play by the rules now that he was in such a strange place. "Okay, Your Highness. If you don't mind, I'd love to use your phone to contact my friends so they can bring me back to the present."

"He dresses in a strange way, and he speaks strange things," the queen observed, and everyone agreed. "What is a phone, stranger? And where are your friends?"

"My friends are in Dark Woods in England. Where are we?"

"He is insane, Your Highness," one of the soldiers said. "He is crazy. He says he can speak to people in England from Egypt."

"Of course I can! I'll use my phone!" Jack snapped, irritated.

"What is a phone?" the queen asked again.

"You do not know what a phone is, Your Highness? There is no network here," Jack said, removing his phone. He turned it so that the screen faced the queen.

"What is that? It's not gold, neither is it diamonds...but it shines like a strange jewel," the queen said.

"Indeed it does," one of the girls standing beside the queen said.

Jack heard a laugh he recognized instantly. It was Half Penny. How could Half Penny be here? Then he heard Amelia's voice, and Eliot's. He also heard Eliot ask: "Is it working, Jack?"

It was as if he could hear his friends inside the city hall but could also hear and see these ancient people through the time machine.

"Strange clothes and strange equipment you have, Stranger," one of the soldiers said. He felt the texture of Seth's jeans with his fingers. "What a heavy and strange garment," he said. "And his feet are shod with a strange footwear," he pointed at the sneakers. "Do such things exist in Greece, or Rome?"

"He is a spy!" another soldier spoke harshly. "Your Highness, if I may be permitted, I will kill this spy!"

Jack watched, horrified as the soldier came towards him, his hand holding what looked like a very sharp sword. Then suddenly Jack was back in the hall with his friends. Eliot had turned the dial on the clock back to the present.

Jack was back in the room of ancient technology with his friends.

"You just saved my life!" he gasped.

"Really? How?"

"I was about to be murdered by an acnie4nt Egyptian soldier and I saw a famous Egyptian queen who lived in 51 BC," Jack said. "It works. That time machine works. And I could hear your voices too. Where is Amelia?"

"She passed out. She's outside. She's been hallucinating since she drank from this bottle," Tom said, and returned the bottle to the shelf. "So the machine really works? What other amazing technology is in this room?"

"What's this? Looks like a giant voltmeter," Tom said, turning the old rusty knob. The glass was very sturdy, and beneath it was a white screen with numbers and a red stick. When he turned the knob, the red stick within the glass turned towards zero and their phones began to make some static sounds. Then Eliot saw that his phone now showed that there was no available network.

"Whatever it is it seems to affect electronics," he said. Later on they would learn that when he turned the knob all TV sets, radios, phones, automatic car controls and all electronics had been affected for those few seconds.

"Let's go. This is a room we'll need to investigate later," Eliot said. But when they stepped out and walked into the room where Amelia had been they noticed that she had vanished.

Amelia was still hallucinating and could not tell if what she was seeing was real or imaginary. Right now she could not decide whether to face the angry bull or the man with the sword, but she knew she had to decide very quickly. Both were coming at her from each of the two passages that led to this place that looked like a barn. She was no matador, but it seemed that even a matador would be scared of a bull this angry, foaming at the mouth and coming toward her like an angry

61

living rocket. Nor was it any more encouraging to see the angry ultra-muscular sword-man. He was dressed in a Black skin garment that ran over one shoulder, leaving one shoulder bare and running down to his knees.

At the very last possible moment, she threw herself flat and rolled away as the bull and the sword-man crashed into the wooden barn wall with incredible force, bringing it down. She struggled to her feet, but as she turned to where the barn wall had been she gaped at the circle of people surrounding her, her focus especially on one man with a head-dress that made him look like a chief. Where was this?

Now she saw that the chief was in fact Half Penny, and he was laughing at her.

"No one has drunk from that bottle in one thousand years," he said to her. She tried to sit up and tried to summon some power, but she was still weak and dizzy.

"I've got an idea. You kids are less trouble when you have had a sip from that drink. I'll give it to your friends as well."

Then she woke up and saw Tom and Eliot staring down at her.

Chapter 11

THE VOODOO DOLLS

They decided to take some of the devices, believing that they could help uncover billions of questions unanswered.

As they continue to walk through the abandoned building, they heard a noise coming from everywhere around them and immediately everyone was ready with their powers and weapons ready for an attack as they continued walking slowly through the hallways. Each of them kept guard on each side. They had vowed to themselves to put an end to the mysterious happenings and make sure that justice would be served. This was something they could only fight with their powers and the knowledge they had about these happenings, and the police would be helpless when it came to stopping Half Penny and whatever other character came along.

Amelia's voice quivered as she called out meekly, "Hello, who's there?"

Eliot shouted as he challenged: "Jacob, if that's you I've got a loaded paint ball gun rifle and I don't miss very often!"

This threat was interrupted by an eerie voice along with laughter and hysterical giggles. For a moment the voice broke into a song. "I am a friend, you will play with me, we will have fun. We have a vendetta against those who wronged us!" Then more rolls of thunderous laughter that echoed all around the building.

"Stop singing right now!" Tom ordered snarled in utter infuriation. His eyes were turning red due to the anger he felt in his mind. His heart beat so fast he feared that it would jump out of his rib cage. He was always a little more impatient compared to the rest of the gang. The voice seemed to mock Tom even more. This time round it mimicked Tom's voice.

"Stop singing right now! Ha ha ha. Like that is ever going to happen! Ha; you make me laugh!" then came more thunderous chuckles.

The voodoo dolls giggled and chuckled insanely.

As the laughing began to intensify and the group formed a circle around each other to be ready for whatever was about to attack them in the hallway and as Amelia's fingers and eyes glowed in blue light, she said, "wait a second" and shot a lightning ball of blue electricity into the air for light see what was going to attack them that day of horror. They then saw the voodoo dolls Eliot and Tom had mentioned last Halloween when they were in the mirror dimension. They were shocked and horrified and got their weapons ready for whatever the evil voodoo dolls were about to do. At that moment the voodoo dolls were standing all over the walls giggling maniacally.

Amelia said in a shaky voice, "Okay, that's creepy."

The voodoo dolls continued laughing and giggling, but this time there was a menacing undertone to the laughter.

At that moment they began to fall off the wall and attacking them with a force that threw them to the ground. It was as if they possessed a power far beyond their size. At the moment the voodoo dolls were about to suffocate Luna by wrapping their hands tightly against her neck, Robin Good, Sam Simon, Lucy and Jack's sister Sera Normans came to help them. They did not understand how Lucy and Sera came to be with Robin Good and Sam, but help was very welcome at this point. Robin and Sam blasted the voodoo dolls and shot them with their weapons and magic powers and fighting skills together and were getting the upper hand - or so they thought until a voodoo doll stabbed Robin Good in the eye with the needle all the way to the back of his head. He groaned in pain and terror and lay dying as the voodoo doll ran away with pearls of laughter. The group were deepest, and they begged Luna to use her powers to help him, as Luna used all of her powers to heal him and it worked, but he could only see through one eye from now on.

Robin Good was a very good friend of theirs ever since he helped rescue Jenny Clark, an imprisoned woman they had found in a house, and ever since he had told them that he was dedicated to stopping Half Penny and undoing all the harm Half Penny was doing. Robin Good's sole mission was to undo all the evil Half Penny did, but he was not as powerful as Half Penny and Half Penny always seemed to be a step ahead, doing more harm than Robin Good could ever undo.

"How is Jenny Clark doing, Robin Good?" Amelia asked.

"Oh, she's doing very well. Half Penny tried to imprison her again, but I was able to frustrate all his efforts."

Robin Good now grunted and groaned in pain. "What ... ow! What happened to me?"

Everyone laughed. "It worked!"

The voodoo dolls had vanished.

At that moment Jack was so overcome with happiness he hugged Luna. She seemed to be very surprised, and there was a very awkward moment after that about it. Luna looked at Jack shyly as she brushed off her hair from her face. There was a very shy grin on her face, one that looked so perfect on her to reveal two beautifully aligned dimples.

"God, she is so beautiful," Jack said to himself.

"Thank you, Jack," Luna said. Jack wondered to himself, "Did I say that out loud?"

For a couple of minutes, there was a long spell of silence as they looked into each other's eyes. There seemed to be some sort of magnet drawing them closer to each other.

"Ahem!" Tom cleared his throat. This caused a distraction between the two and Tom smiled sheepishly as he had cleared his throat to intentionally break the silence that had befallen everyone. Jack and Luna drew back from each other. There were sly laughs and winks from the group.

Jack said in a rather abashed manner: "Luna, um, can we act like that never happened?"

Luna replied, "Yeah, that never happened," and when she noticed that everyone else was looking at her, she blushed even more.

Tom said, "Oh, that's nice! Jack, maybe I should make you two a nice candle light dinner tonight?" Jack gave him a dig in the side with his elbow.

As they were walking back outside to the arcade Jack took Tom to the woods for a private talk.

Jack seemed to be a bit puzzled as he asked, "What does candle light dinner mean?"

Tom seemed confused, wondering what he was talking about. Jack repeated: "What did you mean when you mentioned a candle light dinner when I was with Luna?"

Tom laughed. "Luna seems to be into you, Jack."

Jack yelled in an embarrassed and shocked voice, "What?! I'm afraid I don't understand girls very well…but how can, you be sure?"

"These things happen, but you have to be subtle about them. Don't be too eager to please nor too slow to act. Ladies hate that," Tom said.

"Really?" asked Jack.

"Yes, really. There is a lot more to learn about women. Lucky for you I happen to have a lot of knowledge when it comes to this."

"Well, I truly am in luck as I know little about girls, and I never understand them half the time. So I don't think I would know how to treat a girlfriend – if Luna became my girlfriend."

"Bro, a bird cannot learn to fly unless it flaps it wings. And, besides, still on the example of the bird, no matter how many times it falls to the ground it always keeps trying to fly till it makes it. Same thing with humans."

"I'm not sure I understand you but whoa, I dint know you possess that kind of knowledge and wisdom."

They re-joined the others. They continued walking to the arcade. On arrival, they were continuing playing games.

But at that moment Jack, Luna and Amelia had a vision about the Mirror Dimension and all they saw was two electrical storms making the shape of demons roaring and for some reason they were pissed off at them all and Jack, Luna and Amelia screamed in fear and horror as they saw the living storm enteritis.

Lucy asked with concern: "Are you, okay? I was leaving one of my classmate's place when the next thing I knew Robin Good was holding my hand and I was here." As she finished, she put her hand on their shoulders.

Luna breathed hard. "Um … yeah, I'm okay, speaking for myself."

67

Lucy turned to the others. "Are you okay, Jack and Amelia?"

Amelia and Jack nodded. "Yeah, we're okay."

The others thought they were okay as they were traumatized by the lightning monsters they had envisioned.

Chapter 12

EVIL AND HORROR

Back home at the Tickers', a TV new bulletin caught their attention, and they stopped the card game they were playing. It was about someone who had been killed about one hour ago by a voodoo doll by being stabbed right in the neck, face and chest twenty times by a butcher knife. That was the witness statement anyway.

"You say that the dead man was stabbed by what appeared like a voodoo doll?"

"Yes; that's right," the woman said, looking dazed and shocked.

"But how is that possible? Was the doll alive?"

"Have you ever seen those horror movies with a voodoo doll that has a needed stuck to it? Well, his one had a knife stuck in it. It removed the knife and stabbed the man."

"Did anyone else witness this?"

"No, I was the only one in the grocer where I sell vegetables and fruits and stuff like that when the man came in. The next thing I knew this doll was stabbing him. I didn't see it vanish as I was paralyzed with shock staring at the man as he lay on the floor dying. I can't step inside my grocer again, ever." And she shuddered.

The interviewer turned helplessly back to face the screen. "You heard it from the horse's mouth, Valerie," he said to the newscaster at the station. "Apparently a voodoo doll stabbed the victim to death."

The woman who had been interviewed as a witness was then taken away by two police officers.

"No one will believe her. The police may charge her with murder," Jack said.

The group were worried and decided to go to the mental hospital and see the man who had released Half Penny from his book and get some help from him and see if he had the book because if he had opened it then maybe he still had it.

Eliot said, "Maybe we should go to the Raven Sparrows Mental Hospital where they are holding him?"

Luna had another idea. "Will they allow us to go in to a mental hospital? I think they screen everybody who visits, and only close relatives may be allowed. Maybe, Amelia, Jack and I can go and get him?"

As Luna, Jack and Amelia were teleported by Luna to the morgue in Raven Sparrows Mental Hospital and as they walked slower and slower through the hallways, a woman with a gurney was coming and they heard her footsteps echoing. Jack ran and hid in a closet room and Amelia walked through the walls to the next room and Luna turned invisible to avoid detection and to avoid getting arrested. They were undetected but as they disabled the security cameras the guards became suspicious about what was happening.

Mike the chief guard stared into his screen as it went blank. He noticed that all the screens at the security desk had gone screen.

He said in an angry tone: "Crap! Attention everyone, what's up with the cameras? Either we have a technical problem, or we have intruders?!"

"But what would an intruder want here in the morgue?" one of the other guards asked.

In the evidence room they found one of the magic books and it was titled "Beware of Half Penny's Retribution" and Luna signalled with her hand and told Jack and Amelia to keep an eye out encase if anyone came. She grabbed the book, and they heard echoing footsteps and saw that there were guards coming. Luna hurriedly told them to hold hands, but Jack was still uncomfortable holding hands with Amelia and Luna, but did, nevertheless. She ran with them at superfast speed to the man who had released Half Penny and told them that his name was Alan Morrice. It was then Jack realized that the time travel powers from the ancient time travel machine had not left him. He was able to go back in time to the time Alan Morrice had been alive and asked him about what happened when he opened the book. He explained that when he and his friends were walking down the alley, they heard whispers saying "open the book" and it appeared to them and they opened it and Half Penny crawled out of the book and attacked and murdered them. It was the most traumatic and horrible thing, and he couldn't even imagine about the death and what he had seen Half Penny do to them, and he showed them that Half Penny had stabbed him in the eye with a knife. The guards were outside the room, but right when they opened the door, they were suddenly gone but Alan was still there in this room.

Luna, Amelia and Jack were panting as they came back.

Eliot asked, "Did you get the book?"

At that moment Jack, Luna and Amelia heard a high-pitched sound and heard Jacob's voice singing: "Want to play a game! And even though they believed he was gone and dead he began telepathically talking to them in their mind when he was using the power of telepathy.

Jacob asked in a distorted and dark voice: "Did you think that Amelia and you would be enough to kill me?" Jack grunted. "I thought you were dead, Jacob? Where the hell are you?"

Jacob said: "I think you know exactly where I am and exactly what I'm going to do tonight."

Luna replied: "We are not going to let you hurt our friends!" There was anger in her voice; she sounded really mad.

Possessed Jacob spoke again in that strange way that sounded like Jacob and yet different. "The times for you to stop me from doing anything is over. I'm stronger than you, I'm better than you, and when I'm done with you there won't be anything left, just blood and me with all of your powers remaining after tonight!"

Jack angrily said to Jacob, "You want us to have a show down? All right; let's do this!" And Possessed Jacob replied: "if you think you can beat the crap out of me, then meet me at the city hall tower!"

Amelia, still looking very angry with Jacob, asked: "Do you mean the one where we kicked Half Penny's butt?"

And possessed Jacob laughing in a creepy and evil tone and replied: "First of all, you were hallucinating and were totally helpless. I messed up that drink and made you drink it through mind control, you idiot. And I wanted to destroy that time machine you found among the ancient devices so Jack would be stuck in 51 BC. You are lucky I was distracted. This night is going to end very differently."

"Why are you speaking as if you are Half Penny? You are Jacob!" Luna said, bewildered.

"Shut up!" Possessed Jacob snapped and as he walked back to the city hall tower, Jack, Luna and Amelia told them that Jacobs was back and was at the city hall tower.

Eliot questioned them, saying; "but I thought you said he died?"

Sam replied, "Who's Jacob?"

Luna explained with a sigh, "Jacob is this kid who wrote the book that released a monster from another dimension full of nothing but evil and horror, pure uncorrupted, ancient evil and he has dark magic and has a mysterious past behind him. He's beginning to sound more and more like Half Penny the monster, and it's very creepy. But creepy is something we are getting used to."

Tom then asked, "What's wrong?"

Jack replied in a panicked voice: "Well, he's back, he's at the tower and he said he's going to destroy this world starting with Dark Woods and he wants to kill all of us!"

Lucy then said, "Okay, well, let's go. But are you sure we can beat him?"

Luna looked thoughtful when she said "I don't really know, maybe."

Jack desperately pointed out, "Well, Amelia and I did kill him once … maybe all of us can stop him?"

As they got all their power, weapons and fighting skills ready they walked to the city hall to end it where it all began last Halloween. Meanwhile at the tower possessed Jacob and Cloey were gathering their army of evil voodoo dolls and getting ready to murder them all when the gang arrived.

Amelia shivered. "This place still looks more terrifying than it did last year, and it still gives me the creeps and makes me feel very uncomfortable!" And she shivered again.

Everyone shushed her.

"Be quiet."

"Hey, we are trying to be stealthy here, Amelia!"

Tom whispered, "keep it down Amelia, they could be anywhere?!"

Amelia was annoyed at being silenced like that and snapped back: "Alright, whoa, sorry!"

But at that moment they began to hear bangs, laughter, footsteps and growls and snarls coming from everywhere. Then the light began to blink off and on while glowing green and making thunder bangs and sounds. At that moment they had another encounter with the evil voodoo dolls and Robin Good, who had joined them, was enraged to see the dolls again that dark night of great darkness.

As the dreaded voodoo dolls began to crawl all over them and restrained them to the ground, Possessed Jacob and Cloey showed up and Tom figured out that Jacob was controlling the voodoo dolls with his mind now, which traumatized and upset the gang and Possessed Jacob said, "well, well, well. Amelia, I see you're not alone. Well, neither am I."

As they were all chained to electrified chains, Sam said with a sigh, "how is he doing this? And his pale skin is very scary, but I think he has the devil's eyes - doesn't that creep you out?"

Luna answered, "He has dark powers, remember, so he can have any power he imagines. And yes, it is very creepy and terrifying."

Sam said admiringly, "Whoa, okay, that is actually very amazing and awesome!"

At that moment Amelia's fingers glowed blue and she used her electro kinetic powers to break the chains and freed everyone. Sam was amazed that she could do that.

Amelia whispered, "Come on, and keep quiet and keep an eye out, okay?"

Eliot nodded. "Okay, get the gear."

Tom said, "Here you go, everyone; weapons, equipment, you name them."

As the gang all got their weapons and gear back, they all decided to split into teams.

Tom spoke again. "If Jacob is here, we have to find us before death takes up. Okay, I'll go with Lucy and Jenny. Sam, you go with Robing Good – he uses his power for good and not evil. Luna, you go with Jack and Eliot, and that leaves one team of Sera and Amelia; okay, let's do this."

As Amelia and Sera were walking slowly through the building looking for Jacob with their ears and eyes open and their weapons and powers ready for what would come next, Amelia was talking about hanging out after this and Sera said that she would love to spend time with her as she found Amelia to be a very intriguing person. They heard a bang coming from behind them and when they turned around, they found nothing but a bookshelf. When they banged into it, it sounded hollow and as they thought that it was nothing, but an illusion Amelia spotted and sensed an electrical pulse coming from behind the bookshelf. She then used her power of intangibility to walk through the bookshelf. She found a staircase and tripped over, rolled downstairs into the semi darkness and found a room full of butchered, dead, brutally murdered, blooded bodies hanging all over the room. Amelia screamed in shock and terror. Meanwhile in the hallways Tom, Jack and Luna were walking in the hallways entering a room full of statues of the people who were considered the founders of Dark Woods and Eliot asked in a scared and curious tone where Jacob was. Luna told Eliot to keep quiet because he could have been hiding anywhere behind the statues.

Chapter 13

DEADLY POWERS

Making their way through the empty room, they searched each place their eyes could view. With terror in their hearts, each time they would uncover parts of the statues they would fear one of the dolls would jump out. Limited movements had to be made and communication was non-verbal.

Finally, Luna broke the silence, speaking to Elliot: "I cannot take it anymore; I feel like I am in the middle of a horrible dream that never ends. My heart is beating so fast that I feel it will rip through my chest. My anxiety levels have been off the roof. Why does he keep toying with us? He should just face us since he is 'more powerful' than us. I think they are trying to wear us out and get us to be highly paranoid that he is still around. Once we drop our guard and conclude that they are gone, they will attack us."

In a calm voice, Elliot responded, "I understand what you are feeling. I am in a similar position, but we cannot let him get into our heads. All this is meant to wear us down and get us fighting and questioning each other's ideas. Let us stick together and keep on searching. We came here with one mission and that was to stop him. We cannot let these sideshows distract us. It has to end today, and balance needs to be restored."

At this moment, Elliot and Luna were both in agreement. Sitting on one of the boxes in the room, they decided to take a break before meeting up with the rest of the gang. With a renewed spirit, they were ready to take on Jacob and Cloey.

"Well, well, well, wasn't that an inspirational talk?" came a voice from behind them.

In frantic shock they turned and rose up, seeing Jacob and Cloey hovering in the air.

"I never saw you as an intelligent person, Luna, but I have to give you credit. You have seen through my game plan, and I can see that it is working. You are cracking bit by bit. You have never been one for challenging situations and even though you act tough you are a big coward deep down," said Jacob, still sounding like Half Penny in that weird way. They had already noticed that both Jacob and Cloey had a strange look in their eyes.

"I am not a coward, you called us for this fight, and we will destroy both of you."

Jacob and Cloey burst out laughing maniacally.

Offended by the taunting, Luna shot out laser beams from her eyes at Jacob. He let the laser beams pass through his body and shot it back, but Luna was quick to dodge the shot.

"It seems the party has begun; shall we dance my darling?" said Jacob with an evil grin and the evilest mischief in his eyes.

Luna shot out more beams, but Jacob was too quick for her dodging each shot she would make at him.

Meanwhile, Cloey and Elliot were having a party of their own. Standing on top of one of the statues, she shot an electrical current at Elliot through her fingers. Elliot attempted to take the current into his body and shoot it out like Jacob did, but he lacked the power to do so, and it ended up throwing him to the end of the room.

Cloey jumped from the statue and shot a ray of electricity towards Elliot as he was gaining his consciousness. The electrical current run through Elliot's body as he writhed in pain. At this point Cloey was shooting a consistent beam of electric current to eliminate Elliot from the picture.

Shouting in pain, he gained the attention of Luna, but she couldn't take her eyes off Jacob as he was hot on her heels. Screaming for help, Luna caught the attention of Amelia and Sera who were in a room nearby viewing the dead bodies Jacob had stored.

Luna shot a laser beam at a statue near Jacob as a distraction then shot another beam at Cloey to stop her from killing Elliot.

"I see you have been practicing, dear friend; I will give you credit for that," said Possessed Jacob in a sarcastic tone.

The laser beam Luna shot at Cloey did not deter her from pursuing her mission of killing Elliot. She was good at keeping promises, and today she had come with one mission, to kill and she would see it through to the end.

"You all came here tonight thinking you will end us, but I am so sorry; it will be your funeral today. My day of victory has come," said Possessed Jacob as he let out a loud evil laugh that awakened more voodoo doll's powers.

The party was getting interesting with Luna showing her skills and trying her best not to get killed and not to let Elliot get killed. They had waited for this day with anxiety and fear of what would happen but here it was, and they needed to be brave.

Elliot had gotten wounded badly; he was bleeding on the left side of his stomach, and his strength was waning. "I told you I would win; I always do. You are a weakling hiding behind your brother's shadow. I overestimated you, I must say - I mean you could do better. Sadly, you will not live long enough to see what you could have done, Elliot," said Cloey as she shot laser beams at Elliot whose body was lying next to the statue twitching in agony.

'Get away from them you possessed child,' shouted Amelia in rage as she activated her werewolf side.

"Here comes the puppy. Seems you want to show off your hairy body. It is okay, I am on for a show, forgive me if I pet you without consent," said Cloey and Jacob in sync as a smirk painted their faces.

With Amelia here, the scene was destined to get messy; she was terrified of this place, damn it! She detested this place, the events that had happened at the tower the previous Halloween was one memory she wanted to erase from her mind.

"You are the cause of all this, Jacob. You have allowed Half Penny to influence you and you have become like him. You think I will let you kill my friends? You brought this upon us, upon the Dark Woods Town. Here we are stuck, not sure if we will make it or not because of you, fighting like cats and dogs with one will and desire: to kill and to win. We want to kill you to protect our city and you are obsessed with killing us to become powerful. You were not powerful, remember that," Amelia told Possessed Jacob as.

Jacob lashed voodoo dolls at Amelia to weaken her and put her down; with him able to control them, he wanted her to beg for pity. He had seen that picture before, and here was the opportunity for Amelia to bow down to him.

"You have the courage to speak to me in that tone, risking your life knowing I would end it in a second if I wanted to?"

"The moment you attacked my friends I earned the right to speak to you in any way I like," Amelia said as she spat on Jacob.

In the Hallways, Cloey was chasing after Elliot whose telepathic powers were working against her to make her fail. Unknown to her, it was a trap; Tom and Lucy were waiting for her. She had crossed the line by hurting their brother and she had to face the consequences.

Tom tried shooting an arrow towards Cloe, but her reflexes were too quick. "An arrow, seriously? You should plan better next time – if there will be a next time. This does not work on me. Oh, it's the other brother. I see you have decided to join your brother in his last moment. Do not tell me you want to die with him," said Cloey, shooting laser beams at Tom.

Chapter 14

A COMMON ENEMY

In the meantime, Detective Sinan had been summoned by his boss, Inspector Rowland. He walked into the office and sat uneasily opposite the inspector.

"So? How's it going? Have to gotten to the bottom of this madness? I won't have some weird mysterious deaths and events happening in Dark Woods. I was on a phone call with the mayor, and he says we have to get to the bottom of this. He thinks there's a serial killer loose and he's probably using some hallucinogen or something to confuse any witnesses that think they have something to report. The stories I'm hearing do not make sense at all. You'd think we are in a science fiction movie or a fantasy world somewhere. There must be an explanation for these things!"

"Sir, I'm afraid so far everything has been totally baffling and I'm yet to get to the bottom of this."

"That's not good enough!" Inspector Rowland banged his fist on the desk so hard his coffee spilled on top some papers, and this did not help improve his mood in the least. "No more excuses! Someone's playing tricks and I want you to find out who it is and how they are doing it. What clues do you have?"

"Let's see. Based on witness statements … some mysterious journals, but I have not managed to lay my hands on any of them. A mysterious grotesque puppet that seems to terrify anyone that sees it. I thought I had a lead when I visited some kids who were making some weird noises and playing around with lights, but I'm sure they were just being funny and trying to scare the neighbors. But I'll keep my eye on them… I think they may have seen something, or they may know something. It's just that these things are not rational. Oh, and there's haunted house too."

"A haunted house! Have you lost your mind, Detective?" the inspector gave him an icy scare.

"Abandoned house with weird noises."

"I don't want fairy tales. I want answers, not tales. In the next seven days I need a report that makes sense, not ridiculous speculations."

Detective Sinan unhappily got up and walked out.

Eliot thought he heard an eerie whispering voice say, "Eliot, kill them."

"What who or what said that?" Eliot stammered, looking around in fear

Jack looked concerned. "Hey, Eliot, you okay?" as he noticed Eliot looked scared"

Eliot said, "Yeah, I'm okay … just hearing voices."

But even so, they though because as they heard Amelia scream, and they jumped up. As they fast as fast as they could they ran through the hallway and met up with Lucy and Jenny and continued to investigate the scream. They came to where Sera and Amelia had been, and they saw Sera trying to open the bookcase, but it wouldn't open at all. They all pulled it, but nothing happened; the bookcase wouldn't even shake. Luna's necklace glowed green and red, her eyes and hands began to glow green, and she channelled her power and shot a huge green lightning bolt at the bookcase, and it exploded into a million pieces. As they ran down the stairs they screamed and whimpered in terror and shock as they saw a whole lot of victims chained to the walls and they could tell that it looked like someone had brutally butchered murdered them. They were terrified and couldn't imagine Jacob doing these horrible things – murdering people in cold blood. As they walked to the office room, they found Amelia whimpering and sobbing in the office chair and comforted her to calm her down.

Sera said, "Amelia, it's okay, it's okay."

Amelia was crying and sobbing in fear. "No, it isn't. It's terrifying."

Jacob said in a distorted and sinister voice" "Hello everyone." He chuckled. "I see you have found my shrine of the lost. Great work isn't it. So, I assume you would like to have an end to this story, hmm?"

Robin Good growled. "You stay away from us, you little piece of crap!!!"

As Robin Good attempted to stab Possessed Jacob right in the eyes, Possessed Jacob used telekinesis to freeze Robin and threw him to the next room upstairs. Robin gave a scream of pain. As the rest of the gang attempted to attack Jacob with brute force, he froze them in telekinesis and told them that if they wanted to kill him, they should meet him at the top of the tower and then it would be over. Possessed Jacob teleported away, and the lights banged like lightning, and making thunder sounds and glowing green. The group were enraged and made themselves to the top of the city hall tower to confront Jacob and end the massacre of death around Dark Woods.

As they arrived at the top of the tower, they saw that Possessed Jacob was waiting for them and as the fight began, he turned into his storm form and said, "I should have killed you in the arcade!" but the gang were getting the upper hand because when possessed Jacob turned back to his human state Luna and Amelia combined both of their power together to shoot a massive energy blast at him. It didn't work though. They lost because he blocked and neutralized the blast with one hand, and the power of Luna and Amelia's blast and Jacob blocking it was so powerful it created a huge energy pulse wave and sent an energy wave across the whole city, which shocked Amelia and Luna after they awoke from temporary unconsciousness.

"It's impossible," Luna gasped." No one could do that!"

At that moment Possessed Cloe appeared out of red lightning and attacked and fought the gang. The gang were terrified to see another person with powers like Luna, Amelia and Jacob but they were more scared to see her red and black eyes and pale skin.

"Both of them have got the devil's eyes. They are the devil itself," Robin said with conviction.

Possessed Jacob said: "Where are my manners? Everyone met Cloe Samson, a person with incredible power like me, Amelia and Luna. Cloe's power can pack quit a hell of a punch." As he spoke Possessed Jacob and Cloe combined their powers to shoot a huge lightning blast at the gang, who did the same, both powers colliding with each other. It made a huge shockwaves across the area. As Possessed Jacob and Cloe summoned the voodoo dolls they ambushed and captured the gang. The gang were pinned to the ground as Half Penny revealed himself to them and said, "This time I have won!"

Tom said curiously, "but that's not Jacob's voice."

Half Penny said, "No, it's your other old friend," and he giggled, which terrified Amelia.

"It's really Half Penny!" she said, realising that it wasn't Jacob who was doing these things but Half Penny who was behind it and that he had possessed Jacob and Cloe.

Luna became enraged and upset, knowing that her best friend Jacob had been possessed by the demon puppet who she saw during the scarecrow attack from five days ago. She released a huge energy surge of lightning and somehow it actually separated Half Penny from both Jacob and Cloe, which really pissed off Half Penny and ordered his army of voodoo dolls to kill them all at once. But as Cloe and Jacob awoke from unconsciousness and used their supernatural powers, they all fought Half Penny. As the fight continued, Jacob asked Tom to give him the book.

They were ready to trap Half Penny back in the book, but he grabbed Luna and threatened to slice her throat. He demanded that they go into the mirror dimension. As Jacob stepped towards Half Penny, he quickly opened the book on Half Penny again and Half Penny gasped and yelled "what?!"

Jacob shot Half Penny with a purple lightning bolt and Half Penny grabbed Luna's right hand. Luna screamed and Jacob quickly grabbed her left hand and grunted in pain. The gang held on to her hand and painfully but successfully pulled her back to the real world. Half Penny screamed in rage, "No! Not again!" as he disappeared back into the mirror dimension where he belonged along with the voodoo dolls.

Jacob slammed the book shut and put it in his pocket for safe keeping. As Jacob and Cloe were about to walk off into the night Amelia stopped him.

"Jacob. I'm sorry. We all are. We really thought you had gone completely rogue and had no idea that Half Penny had possessed you and was using you to do his dirty work," she said.

"Yes, sorry, Jacob. I had begun to think this was your endgame and that this had been your plan all along. Make friends with us, pretend to work with us against Half Penny and then try to destroy us all and then destroy the whole town."

"We cannot allow Half Penny to divide us," Luna said. "If we are to make sure Half Penny is completely destroyed and that there are no journals out there to cause more havoc we must work together. When we are divided Half Penny can easily defeat us. Did you see how he used your power against us instead of that power being used to defeat him, Jacob?"

"Yes, that cunning evil puppet monster is very clever," Jack agreed.

Jacob smiled. "I'm glad we are all friends again," he said. "I really felt very angry at you all, and my only desire was to destroy you. He really had taken control of my mind."

"Mine too," Cloe said.

"You can be our friend too, Cloe," Amelia smiled. "She can, can't she?"

"Of course! You were being used just like Jacob," Lucy agreed.

"I have known Cloe since I was a child. We grew up together. You will like her," Jacob grinned. Then he became serious. "We must be very careful. The police are already wondering what we have been up to and what we know, even though they don't really know about Half

Penny. That detective is smart, but he has no idea what's really been going on. We cannot afford to work against other when we have a common enemy – Half Penny and the dark world of the mirror dimension."

As they were walking happily back to their houses getting ready for what would come next, they decided the first thing they would do that night was to have some fun and rest.

The End.